DREAMWORKS®
MEGAMIND™
BAD. BLUE. BRILLIANT.

MAKE YOUR OWN COMIC STICKER BOOK

PSS!
PRICE STERN SLOAN

An Imprint of Penguin Group (USA) Inc.

DreamWorks' Megamind: Bad. Blue. Brilliant. ™ & © 2010 DreamWorks Animation L.L.C. Published by Price Stern Sloan,
a division of Penguin Young Readers Group, 345 Hudson Street, New York, New York 10014.
PSS! is a registered trademark of Penguin Group (USA) Inc. Printed in the U.S.A.

ISBN 978-0-8431-9923-9   10 9 8 7 6 5 4 3 2 1

HOW TO DRAW MEGAMIND

Megamind is the smartest villain of all time. But with great knowledge comes a great big brain . . . and a great big head to hold that brain!

Using a separate piece of paper, follow these steps to learn how to draw this evil villain!

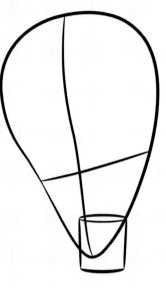

Step One

Draw a teardrop shape for Megamind's face. Lightly draw guidelines through the middle of the shape so you will know where to place his features. Then add a cylinder to the bottom of Megamind's face for his neck.

Step Two

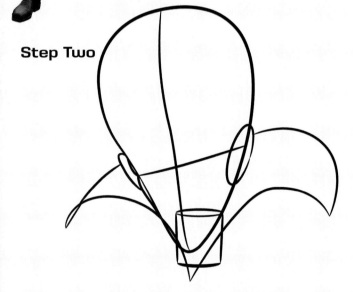

Add a crescent shape to the right side of Megamind's face for his collar. Then draw a triangle with a loop on the point on the left side of his face. This will be the other side of his collar. Finish with a circle on both sides of his face for Megamind's ears.

Step Three

Erase the lines from the cylinder that formed Megamind's neck, as shown. Then add triangles on both sides to complete his collar. Draw two curved lines under the horizontal guideline on Megamind's face for his eyes, a bell shape for his nose, and a curved line for his mouth.

Step Four

Erase the guidelines on Megamind's face, as shown. Add a curved line to give Megamind's nose the proper shape and draw a straight line over each of his eyes. Finally, add two triangles on the right side of Megamind's collar.

Step Five

Erase the lines on the right side of Megamind's collar and on his nose, as shown. Add arched eyebrows and draw in his beard. Then add half circles to Megamind's eyes. Finally, add slightly curved lines to the tops of his ears.

Step Six

Color in Megamind's eyebrows and beard. Add two lines above his eyebrows and two slightly curved lines below them. Then add curved lines below each of Megamind's eyes, smile lines on either side of his nose, and a curved line on the right side of his face. Add curved lines to finish his ears, and two slightly curved lines to finish his collar. Congratulations! You've now drawn Megamind!

CREATE YOUR OWN COMIC

Use your imagination to create your own Megamind comic strip. The sky is the limit when it comes to Megamind and his evil ways: He could have a new invention that promises to destroy Metro City once and for all! Or maybe he's kidnapped Roxanne Ritchi in another attempt to trap Metro Man.

Use your stickers to place each character in the scene and then write your own captions in the balloons.

GOOD VS. EVIL

Look at the puzzle and figure out where each piece fits.

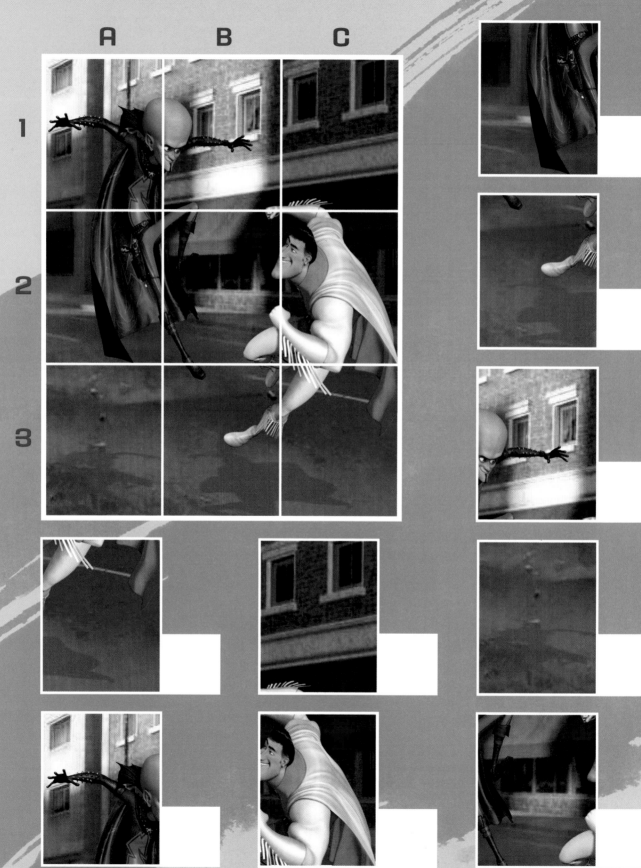

MEET MINION

Look at the image and count the number of squares.

STRIKE A POSE

Metro Man loves to strike a pose for his adoring fans. Here are some of his favorites:

Circle the pose that only appears once.

UP TO NO GOOD

Megamind always has new gadgets up his sleeve to help him take over Metro City.

Connect the pictures with the identical groupings of his evil inventions.

HOW TO DRAW METRO MAN

Metro Man is the world's best superhero. He even has a perfect smile and perfect hair.

Using a separate piece of paper, follow these steps to learn how to draw your very own perfect Metro Man.

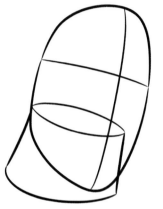

Step One

Draw an oval for Metro Man's face. Lightly draw guidelines through the middle of the shape so you will know where to place his features. Then add a cylinder to the bottom of Metro Man's face for his neck.

Step Two

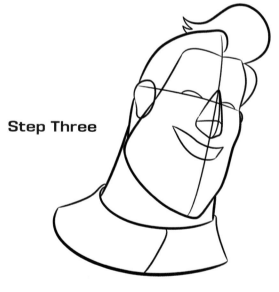

Step Three

Erase the lines for the cylinder that formed Metro Man's neck, as shown. Then add the lines for his collar. Draw an oval shape on the left side of Metro Man's head for his ear and a curved line to the right of his face to give it shape. Finally, add the line for Metro Man's hair.

Erase the guidelines from the oval that formed Metro Man's face, as shown. Then add an upside-down L shape to define his hairline, and a half circle to the right side of his head to finish his hair. Draw two half circles above the horizontal guideline on Metro Man's face for his eyes, add a pyramid for his nose, and add lines for his mouth. Finally, add a curved line to the middle of Metro Man's collar.

Step Four

Erase the guidelines on Metro Man's face, as shown, and add a diagonal line under his left ear. Then draw in his eyebrows and add a curved line for his nose. Add smile lines to Metro Man's face and a curved line for his chin. Then add two buttons to his collar.

Step Five

Erase any unnecessary guidelines, as shown. Then add two curved lines between Metro Man's eyebrows, two straight lines under his eyes, a curved line on his nose, and smile lines on both sides of his mouth. Add two circles in Metro Man's eyes for his eyeballs and curved lines for his teeth. Finally, draw a curved line on his chin and curved lines to finish his ear.

Step Six

Color in Metro Man's eyes. Then add lines through his hair and draw straight lines to separate his teeth. Presto! You have now drawn your very own superhero!

CREATE YOUR OWN COMIC

Ever wonder what the best part about being a superhero is? The adoring fans, of course! But in order to win over a city full of people, a superhero has to show everyone just how super he can be. Whether he is rescuing a cat stuck in a tree or leaping over tall buildings to stop Megamind in his tracks, Metro Man is always in the public eye.

Use your stickers to place each character in the scene and then write your own captions in the balloons.

LIVE FROM METRO CITY

Roxanne Ritchi is Metro City's star reporter. What would a reporter be without a microphone to report the news?

Circle the image of Roxanne in which she doesn't have her microphone.

MEGAMIND'S MASTER PLAN

Megamind has captured Roxanne and is showing her his evil plan. Can you spot the five differences between the two scenes?

WHAT COMES NEXT?

As he soars through the sky, Metro Man hits many striking poses.

Study each row to figure out which pose Metro Man will break out next! Then use your stickers to put the correct pose in the empty circle.

Page 16

Pages 22-23

Extra Stickers

MEGAMIND HAS DONE IT AGAIN!

Megamind has a new invention, but as usual there are some hiccups in the execution! Can you figure out who's who?

A _____

B _____

C _____

D _____

How to Draw Minion

Minion is Metromind's trusty sidekick. He's always there when Megamind needs a right-hand man.

Using a separate piece of paper, follow these steps to learn how to draw Minion.

Step One

Draw an oval for Minion's fish tank. Add a curved line beneath it. Then add another oval inside the fish tank and lightly draw guidelines through the middle of the shape so you will know where to place Minion's features.

Step Two

Step Three

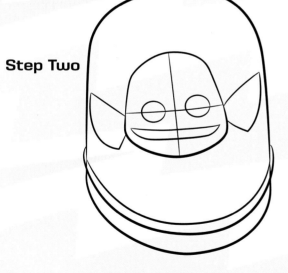

Draw two circles for Minion's eyes and add lines for his mouth. Then add a triangle to each side of his face for his fins. Finally, draw a curved line around the bottom of his fish tank.

Draw a curved line around the top of Minion's head. Then add a second set of circles inside his eyes and another square inside his mouth. Draw curved lines from one end of Minion's fins to the other, as shown. Add squares to each side of his tank, and finish with three sets of lines running from right under Minion's face to the bottom of the tank.

Step Four

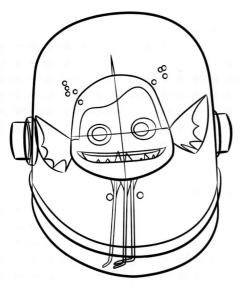

Add circles to the squares on each side of Minion's tank. Then draw more circles above and below his head. Draw triangles for Minion's teeth, a triangle on the top of his head, and three triangles below his head connected to the straight lines. Curve the bottom of the straight lines below Minion's head and close them off, as shown.

Step Five

Remove any unnecessary guidelines, as shown. Then add straight lines to connect the circles you drew in the previous step to Minion's body. Draw more triangles to finish his teeth and add smile lines to the sides of his mouth. Finally, draw two lines above the tank for antennae.

Step Six

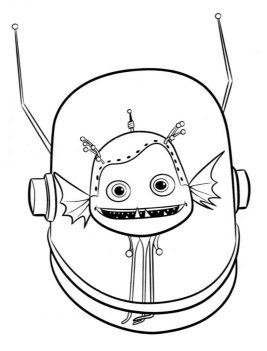

Color in Minion's eyes and mouth. Add black dots along the top of his head and draw lines on his fins. Finally, draw a circle at the top of each antenna and another straight line to connect the other side of his antenna to his head. Minion is now complete!

CREATE YOUR OWN COMIC

As soon as Tighten arrived on the superhero scene, he saw that being bad was way more fun than being good. Now this hero has used his powers to become Metro City's worst villain yet. He destroys buildings rather than protects them, and he lets Metro City citizens fend for themselves when they're in danger!

Use your stickers to place each character in the scene and then write your own captions in the balloons.

Defeat Metro Man once and for all! Jump ahead one space.

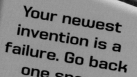

Your newest invention is a failure. Go back one space.

Race around town in your invisible car. Jump ahead one space.

Kidnap Roxanne Ritchi to start a new battle with Metro Man. Jump ahead one space.

START

BAD. BLUE. BRILLIANT. GAME

Play this game with a friend! Place your stickers on a coin and use these as your game pieces.

Place your game pieces at START and take turns moving around the game. On your turn, flip a coin. Move two spaces forward for heads, one space for tails. The first player to make it all the way to FINISH wins!

Put your latest plans to take over Metro City into effect! Jump ahead one space.

Tighten tries to become Metro City's newest villain. Go back one space.

The Brainbots act up. Miss a turn.

Brainstorm a new plan with Minion to put Tighten in his place. Jump ahead one space.

With the help of the Brainbots, Minion, and Roxanne, you defeat Tighten. You are Metro City's newest hero!

FINISH.
YOU WIN!

ANSWERS

Page 6

A2 B3 B1
C3 C1 A3
A1 C2 B2

Page 8

Page 14

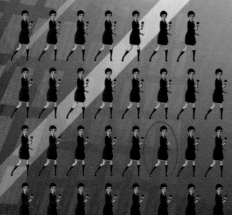

Page 16

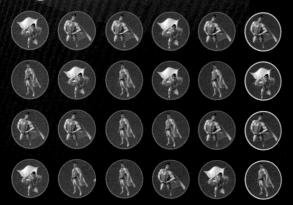

Page 7

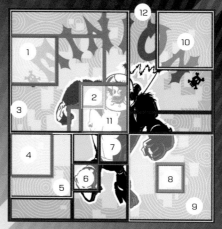

1 12 10
2 11 7
3
4 6 8
5 9

Page 9

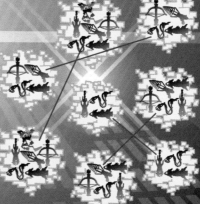

Page 15

Page 17

A. Megamind   B. Metro Man

C. Roxanne   D. Tighten